Dude Dog's Dreams

Dude
the Hunter

Written & Illustrated by Sue V. Daly

Dude

First published by Aquinas & Krone Publishing, LLC 11/16/2011.

ISBN # 978-0-9843526-9-2

This book is printed on acid-free paper.

All illustrations are by Sue V. Daly.
Ms. Daly is also the illustrator of the best-selling "Mookie" series:
"Everybody Loves Mookie" "Mookie and the Rescued Cat" "Mookie Goes Down the Shore"
"Mookie and the Christmas Tree" and "Mookie and the Candy Store".

Please feel welcome to visit www.illustrationsbySueDaly.com & JudithKristen.com

Sue V. Daly's photo taken by Shauna L. Daly.
Cover design by Tim Litostansky.
Edited by Judith Kristen.

A special thanks to my friend Kathy Metcalf for all of her assistance.
This book is dedicated to my adorable twin grandchildren, Emma & Drew.

Hi! My name is Dude and I'm a very sweet, but very ordinary beagle from a lovely place called Barrington, Illinois.

Sometimes my Mom calls me Doodle.

She thinks it's cute.

Frankly, I think it's embarrassing.

Anyway, so where was I?

Oh, yes!

I want you to know that even if I am just your average beagle in the daytime, at nighttime or naptime I'm the King of Adventure – if only in my dreams. And yesterday, I had one of the most interesting dreams in my entire life!

Would you like to hear about it?

You would?

Okay…here it goes!

The minute I fell asleep I heard someone calling to me, "Dude, Dude! Pay attention!"

I turned toward the voice. It was coming from another beagle standing right next to me. "Who are you?" I questioned.

"I'm Corky, The Beagle Boss."

"The Beagle what?"

"The Beagle **Boss**! Now go on over there and get in line behind Charlotte and Ruby. Go on. Get!"

"Okay," I smiled. "You're the boss."

As I looked around to find Charlotte and Ruby I realized that I was in the middle of a very large pack of beagles. There must have been a hundred, or a thousand…or maybe even a million of us…or maybe even…

"DUDE!" Corky shouted. "Once again you're not paying attention! Do your job! Sniff! **Sniff**!!! Put your nose to the ground and **sniff**! What kind of hunting dog are you anyway?!"

"**I'm** a hunting dog? Well what do you know?" I thought to myself, "**I'm** a hunting dog!" All of a sudden I felt very proud and important. "So, what exactly are we hunting?" I asked.

Ruby shook her head at me. "Why fox, rabbit, and deer of course!"

"Oh, of course!" And before you could say fox, rabbit, and deer, I put my nose to the ground and got to sniffing.

I followed Charlotte and Ruby's lead and did exactly what they did. We sniffed and then moved the grass around with our noses.

I thought to myself, "If this is hunting it sure doesn't seem too complicated."

Then all of a sudden the sniffing stopped and we started to run full speed through a bright yellow field. That was so much fun!

We ran up a steep, grassy hill and then down through a large meadow of beautiful wildflowers. They smelled wonderful!

Next we ran across a cool, blue stream. I liked the way the water splashed on my tail and my ears.

THEN…we ran to the deep dark forest.

I stopped right in my tracks. "Uh Oh! I really don't want to go in there."

"What's the matter with you?" Ruby asked.

"Well, see…my mother never lets me go into the forest. She'd be angry with me if I did," I said to Ruby.

Ruby just looked at me and shrugged. "But you're safe, Dude. You're hunting with the pack. You're Mom would be proud, not angry."

I looked into her soft brown eyes. "Ruby, I think you're right. Yep! Mom would be proud. I'm a big boy now!"

Just as I was about to follow my newfound pack into the forest I saw something move to the right of me. Being the curious beagle that I am I slowed down a bit to take a closer look right behind a very big oak tree.

"Hellooooo! Anybody there?"

"Shoo! Go away! Go on, doggie, keep moving!" a voice answered.

I knew the tree wasn't talking to me so I decided to walk just a bit further to see exactly who it was!

    As I rounded the tree, there, peeking through some sparse branches was a very small, red fox with big golden-brown eyes.

    "Don't be scared." I smiled at him. "My name's Dude. I'd never hurt anyone. Who are you? What's your name? Are you lost?"

"To answer your questions, **I** am a fox, my name is Max, and I'm not lost. Now keep going! Please!" he said to me swishing his big bushy red tail.

"You want me to leave?" I asked. "Wouldn't you rather join us? We're going into the forest. It should be a lot of fun!"

"Not for me it won't! Now please just go away," he begged. "They'll see me and then they'll catch me."

"See you? Catch you? Who will?" I asked innocently.

"The hunters, you silly dog. I'm a fox. Hunters hunt fox."

"Oh, that's right," I said puffing out my chest with pride. "You know, **I'm** a hunter! That's how I found you!"

"Well," the fox smiled, "you're not the kind of hunter I'd ever be afraid of, but just go – please."

From the edge of the forest I heard Charlotte calling me.

"Dude, come on, hurry! You have to keep up! What are you doing over there?" She started to run toward us.

"Oh no! Hide me, Dude! Hide me!" Quickly Max jumped right on top of my head.

"I'll be right there!" I called back to Charlotte. "Max my friend, this isn't going to work. Off of my head, little fella." I smiled at him. "It's alright, now."

"Really?"

"Yes, really. And I won't tell anyone you're here."

"Promise?"

"I promise."

"Thanks, Dude! I like you. You're a very kind and thoughtful beagle."

"Why thank you, Max."

    While on the way to rejoin my pack I saw something else move – this time to my left.

    Being the curious beagle that I am, I just had to go over and take a look.

    I tiptoed through some bushes, carefully stepped through some sticker branches, and then tumbled into a huge berry patch. When I looked up I saw two floppy ears, big bright eyes, and a while fluffy tail. It was a rabbit nibbling on a juicy red berry.

"Hi, I'm Dude! What's your name? Do you need help picking berries? What type of berry are they? Are they strawberries? Are they raspberries? They look delicious. Can I pick some with you?" I asked him.

The rabbit quickly turned and in a low quiet voice said, "Hush! My name is Cody, and no I don't need your help. Now go away! Don't stop here, keep moving."

"But why?" I asked.

"Because they'll see me and they'll catch me."

"See you? Catch you? Who will?" I asked innocently.

"The hunters, you silly dog. I'm a rabbit. Hunters hunt rabbit."

"Oh, that's right," I said puffing out my chest with pride once again. "I'm a hunter too, you know. Are you scared of me?"

"Dude," the rabbit smiled, "you're not the kind of hunter I'd ever be afraid of."

"So I've heard. Anyway, I have to go now, Cody. My dog pack is heading deep into the forest so you should be safe right here where you are. No worries."

"Thanks, Dude. It was nice meeting you!"

"It was nice meeting you too, Cody! And enjoy those juicy berries, my new friend!"

    I hurried toward my Beagle pack hollering, "I'm coming, Charlotte and Ruby! I'll be right there!" As I ran deeper and deeper into the forest I heard another unusual sound. I turned to face the direction of the noise but I couldn't quite see anything. Then I looked closer.

And closer...
And closer...

   WOW! Not three feet in front of me, hidden by lots of foliage, was a big beautiful deer chewing on some very large and very crunchy leaves.
   CRUNCH! CRUNCH! CRUNCH!

"Well, hello there, big fella! My name's Dude and I…"

"Shhhhh, go away, keep moving!" he said to me.

"But why?" I asked.

"Because they'll see me and they'll catch me," the deer said.

"See you? Catch you? Who will?"

"The hunters, you silly beagle. I'm a deer and hunters hunt deer."

"Oh, that's right. I keep forgetting. Okay Mr. Deer, I'll move on. Sorry for disturbing your lunch. Have a nice day and enjoy those leaves!"

This hunting game is fun, I thought to myself. I find the animals. Then I keep them safe. And I've made a lot of nice new friends.

As I turned to leave my new deer buddy, I came face to face with Corky, The Beagle Boss. I thought maybe I could hide the big deer but I just couldn't.

Uh-Oh. I'm in big trouble!

But then Corky smiled at me, turned to face the deer and said, "Hey, Charlie, what's up?"

"Hey there, Cork, not much. Just having a chat with my new pal, Dude."

I stood there with my mouth so wide open my whiskers hit the ground!

"You two know each other?"

"I know all of the forest creatures, Dude. They're my good friends. I protect them from the hunters," said Corky.

"Do the other hunting dogs know about this?" I asked.

"Sure! We're friends with everyone in the forest. They're animals just like us! We don't want to hurt any of them."

"So I did a good job?"

"You sure did," Corky smiled at me again. "You're not the best sniffer in the whole world, but you've learned how to make new friends, and how to be a good friend and that's the most important lesson of all. Isn't it Charlie?"

"Indeed it is."

"So, now where to?" I asked Corky.

"Well, this is your dream, Dude. That's up to you."

Just then I heard…

CRASH! CRASH!! BANG!!! BANG!!!!

I awoke to Mom pulling pots and pans from the kitchen cabinet. I stretched and yawned and yawned and stretched. Mom looked at me and smiled. "Sorry, Doodle. Did I wake you from one of your exciting Dude Dreams?"

"How does she know that?"

"Go on back to sleep. We'll be gone for a while. We're taking Emma and Drew to the Aquarium today."

"The Aquarium? How exciting!"

"I'd love to take you with us, Doodle, but no doggies allowed."

I stretched and yawned a bit more and then made myself comfortable back in my nice, soft Beagle bed.

"That's okay, Mom. In my dreams, I'm allowed everywhere."

I closed my eyes and drifted off to sleep once again. And in my next dream…

Can you guess where I was?

I bet you can!

The End

...for now

Sue V. Daly is an award-winning illustrator specializing in pen and ink renderings. She graduated from the University of Pennsylvania, Kutztown, with a degree in Advertising Art. She is the illustrator for the Mookie the Adventure Cat series, written by Judith Kristen. Sue has two daughters, Lauren and Shauna and two grandchildren Emma and Drew. She is a native of New Jersey now living outside of Chicago with her husband Bill and her two beagles Corky and Dude.

Dude Daly was born on June 21st, 2004.

The darling canine author is a totally adorable boy (awake or asleep) and he loves his happy life, his animal friends, and his family, with all of his heart.

Dude's favorite things are: his stuffed brown bear, peanut butter, and following Mom around the house all day, and of course, his dreams!

CPSIA information can be obtained
at www.ICGtesting.com
Printed in the USA
262873LV00002B